SWIM like a FISH

This book belongs to

....

THIS STORY HAS...

Hoot
Jessie's toy owl

Jessie
She lives with her mum, dad and Baby Archie

Archie
Jessie's baby brother

Jessie's mummy

Jessie's dad

The
ticket lady

The
BIG Pool!

Read more books in this series:

Can I Slurp My Spaghetti?

My Turn, Your Turn

Where are you Scruffy Pup?

SWIM LIKE A FISH

A LAUGHING LOBSTER BOOK 978-1-913906-98-6

Published in Great Britain by Laughing Lobster, an imprint of Centum Publishing Ltd.
This edition published 2021.

5 7 9 10 8 6 4

© 2021 Laughing Lobster, an imprint of Centum Publishing Ltd. All Rights Reserved.

Illustrations by Julia Seal.

No part of this publication may be reproduced, stored in a retrieval system, or transmitted in any form or by any means, electronic, mechanical, photocopying, recording or otherwise, without the prior permission of the publishers.

Laughing Lobster, an imprint of Centum Publishing Ltd, 20 Devon Square, Newton Abbot, Devon, TQ12 2HR, UK. Centum Publishing Ltd, 9/10 Fenian St, Dublin 2, D02 RX24, Ireland

books@centumpublishingltd.co.uk

LAUGHING LOBSTER, CENTUM PUBLISHING LIMITED Reg. No. 08497203

A CIP catalogue record for this book is available from the British Library.

Printed in Great Britain.

FSC
www.fsc.org
MIX
Paper from
responsible sources
FSC® C014540

SWIM like a FISH

Let's play hide and seek! Can you find
Hoot the owl hiding in the story 16 times?

Saturday was always swimming day for Jessie and Dad. Jessie loved the small pool and splashing in the shallow water.
But Dad said that this swimming day was going to be different.

"I have a surprise for you," smiled Dad.
Jessie liked surprises.
"Today we're going to swim in the big pool," said Dad.
"The BIG pool – yippee!" shouted Jessie.

Jessie was excited! The BIG pool was just for big girls and boys. She grabbed Hoot and ran to the door. "Hold on," chuckled Dad. "We still have to pack our swimming bag like normal."

So Jessie and Dad packed . . .
two swimming costumes,

two fluffy towels,

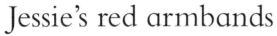

Jessie's red armbands

and a shiny coin for
the locker.

At the Sports Centre, Jessie, Dad and Hoot waited in the queue.

"Two tickets for the BIG pool," said Jessie.

"The big pool!" smiled the lady. "You are grown-up!"

"This way," called Dad as they went into the changing rooms. "This is where we get changed when we go into the big pool," he explained.

"Would Hoot like to wait here?" asked Dad.

"No. Hoot wants to see what the BIG pool is like, too!" cried Jessie.

"OK," smiled Dad. "As long as he waits on the side. He can look after our towels."

Jessie and Dad walked past the little pool to the big pool. Jessie's tummy felt funny now. The big pool was very noisy. She clung tightly to Hoot.

Suddenly the big pool felt very, very big and Jessie and Hoot felt very, very small.

"Let's watch for a while," suggested Dad.
Everyone else in the big pool looked like they were
having fun. There were lots of other children playing
and splashing and swimming all by themselves.

"Shall we go in?" asked Dad.
"I think I want to stay here," replied Jessie. "Hoot is
a bit scared of the big pool."
"I was scared the first time that I went into the
big pool too," said Dad.
"But Dad, you can swim like a fish!" said Jessie.

"I couldn't always. Grandpa helped me," Dad
explained. "He showed me a special game to help me
learn how to swim. It's called 'move like an animal'."
"Move like an animal?" asked Jessie, confused.

Dad climbed down the steps into the water.
"Right, first move . . . would you like to jump like
a frog?" asked Dad.
Dad jumped up in the water. "If you jump then I'll
catch you," he said.

Showers ←
← Changing Rooms
Flumes →

Jessie was still a bit nervous, but jumping like a frog did look fun. She closed her eyes and bent her knees.

One, two, three ... **SPLASH!**

The big pool was very deep, and Jessie couldn't touch the bottom.

"Dad, can we go to the side?" asked Jessie.

"Yes and there we can walk like a crab!" he smiled.

Dad showed Jessie how to move her hands along the edge of the pool. She pulled herself sideways just like a crab.

"Shall we make bubbles like a fish?" Dad suggested.
He dipped his face in the water and blew bubbles.

"I want to blow bubbles like a fish too!" giggled Jessie.
She dipped her face in the water and blew.

Jessie and Dad practised lots of different animal moves together.

They snapped like crocodiles,

stretched like starfish,

bobbed like ducks

and squirted like whales.

By the end of this swimming day, Jessie decided the big pool was very, very fun!

"Well done, Jessie!" said Dad when they had finished.
"You'll soon be swimming like a fish too!"
"Hooray! I can't wait – can we come swimming
tomorrow too?" she giggled.

THE END

What is different about going swimming for Jessie?

Where do Jessie and Daddy put their clothes?

Does Jessie jump straight in the big pool?

What does Jessie wear on her arms to help her swim?

What animal does Jessie pretend to be along the side of the pool?

How does Jessie blow bubbles?

Like a fish!

SAY GOODBYE TO...

Hoot
Jessie's toy owl

Jessie
She lives with her
mum, dad and
Baby Archie

Archie
Jessie's baby brother

Jessie's mummy

Jessie's dad

The
ticket lady

The
BIG Pool!

HOPE YOU ENJOYED
THE STORY!